Crossing the Street

"Coloured Bedtime StoryBook"

By

Thanoudeth Vongkhamsouk

Illustrated by

Nivong Sengsakoune

ILLUSTRATED & PUBLISHED
BY
E-KİTAP PROJESİ & CHEAPEST BOOKS

www.cheapestboooks.com

 www.facebook.com/EKitapProjesi

ISBN: 978-625-6308-90-9

Copyright, 2024 by e-Kitap Projesi

Istanbul

Categories: Problem Solving & Animals
Country of Origin: Laos Republic
Cover: © Cheapest Books
License: CC-BY-4.0

For full terms of use and attribution, http://creativecommons.org/licenses/by/4.0/

Contributing: Nivong Sengsakoune

© **All rights reserved**.

Except for the conditions stated in the License, no part of this book shall be reproduced or transmitted in any form or by any means, electronic or mechanical, including photocopy, recording or by any information or retrieval system, without written permission form the publisher.

About the Book

Toad, Rabbit, and Snail have to cross the street to get to school every day, but Snail is afraid. How will Snail's friends help him get across the street?

Crossing the Street
Thanoudeth Vongkhamsouk
Nivong Sengsakoune

Three friends, Toad, Rabbit, and Snail live near each other in a small village.

This year, Toad, Rabbit, and Snail will go to a new school.

They are happy and excited.

They need to cross the street on the way to the new school. Rabbit and Toad look left then right.

When there are no cars passing by, they quickly cross the street.

But Snail doesn't cross the street.

Toad and Rabbit see that Snail is afraid, so they call out to Snail.

"Careful! Follow us quickly!"

Snail walks slowly. He can't leap as fast as Toad.

He sees a traffic jam in the middle of the road.

Snail feels scared as he crosses the street.

Toad and Rabbit immediately come to his rescue.

Every car stops to allow Snail and his friends to cross the street.

Snail is relieved after he crosses.
Toad and Rabbit yell, "Yay! Snail made it across the street!"

They safely arrive at school.

Snail says, "Wow! Crossing the street was so scary!"

Toad and Rabbit talk together, "What can we do to help Snail safely cross the street?"
They think and think and think some more. Finally they find a way to help Snail cross the street.

After school, Snail rides on the cart that Rabbit and Toad built to help Snail cross the street.

"Wow! I'm so happy.
I can now safely cross the street!"

From that moment on, Snail didn't have issues crossing the street.

End of the Story

www.ingramcontent.com/pod-product-compliance
Lightning Source LLC
LaVergne TN
LVHW070454080526
838202LV00035B/2826